Dream Adventure Series

AFSA

THE MERMAID QUEEN

ADITHYA IYER

BlueRose Publishers

First Published in March 2020

ISBN: 978-93-90034-69-7

BLUEROSE PUBLISHERS

www.bluerosepublishers.com

info@bluerosepublishers.com

+91 8882 898 898

Cover Design:

Vandana Kanyal

Typographic Design:

Tanya Raj Upadhyay

Distributed by: BlueRose, Amazon, Flipkart, Shopclues

AFSA - THE MERMAID QUEEN

Aadhi, Ram and Nidhi were playing at the beach. Nidhi spotted a Mermaid. All three of them went inside the ocean to meet her.

What happened next? Will they come back?

Aadhi had a dream while sleeping

Aadhi, Ram and NIdhi were playing at the beach.

Nidhi saw a Mermaid and was shocked!

"Look! It is a Mermaid!" - said Nidhi

"Is that the one?" - Exclaimed Ram

"Then let us go and meet the Mermaid" - said Ram

"How?" - asked Nidhi

"Uncle Manu will help us" - said Ram

Uncle Manu owns a ship. He trained all three of them in scuba diving and deep-sea diving.

What are you guys doing here? - asked Uncle Manu.

"We spotted a Mermaid and need your help to meet her" - said Aadhi

Interesting! A Mermaid?! I did not believe it when many people told me.

Let us go on my ship. I will help you guys to meet her.

Uncle Manu, Ram, Nidhi, and Aadhi started sailing in the ship to meet the Mermaid.

"There she is!" - said Aadhi, after spotting the Mermaid.

Uncle Manu gave them the masks and oxygen cylinders.

"We all are looking like Astronaut" - said Ram.

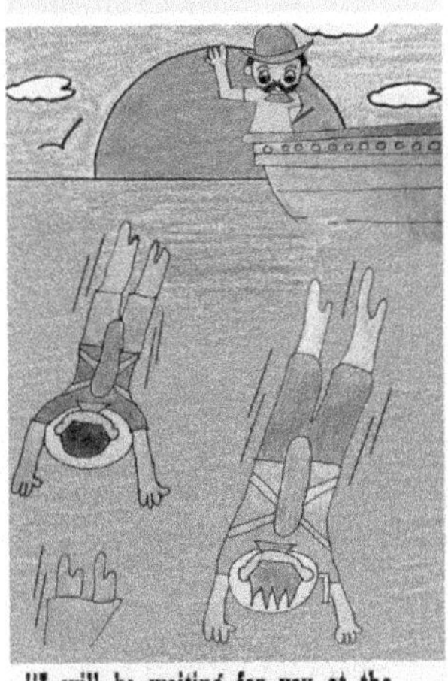

"I will be waiting for you at the beach" - said Uncle Manu

All three of them reached the seabed.

Thanks to Uncle Manu for this suit. Everything is crystal clear! - said Ram.

Hi Kids! My name is Moly. I am your friend.

"Hi, Moly!" - said all three of them

"Hey, Moly! do you know where does the Mermaid live?" - asked Nidhi.

"There she is" - said Ram.

"She is beautiful!" - said Ram
I think these kids do not know about her.
I should ask these kids to leave before the evil Mermaid finds them!.

Moly realized it was too late to ask the kids to leave when she saw the army of Mermaid. Moly understood it was a trap.

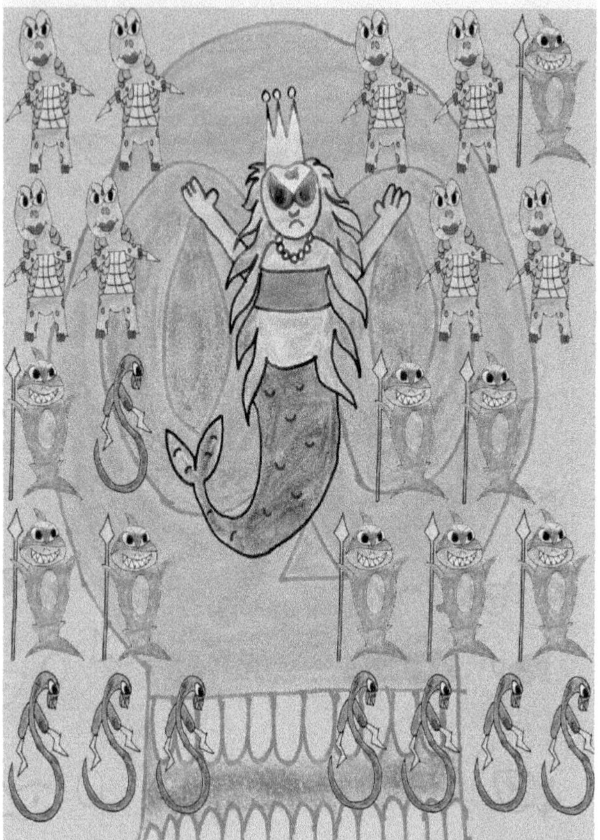

"I am Afsa, the Mermaid Queen. I am here with my army to capture you all. You three will be my servant." - said Afsa

All of them started screaming out of fear!

I should do something before Afsa takes these kids to her castle!.

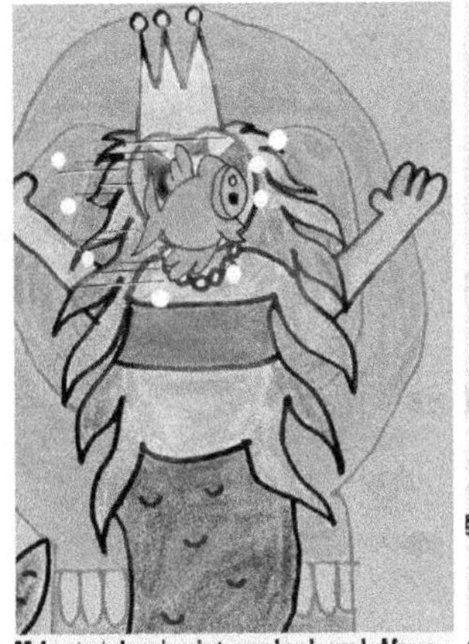

Moly started swimming round-and-round Afsa so that she will not be able to see anything.

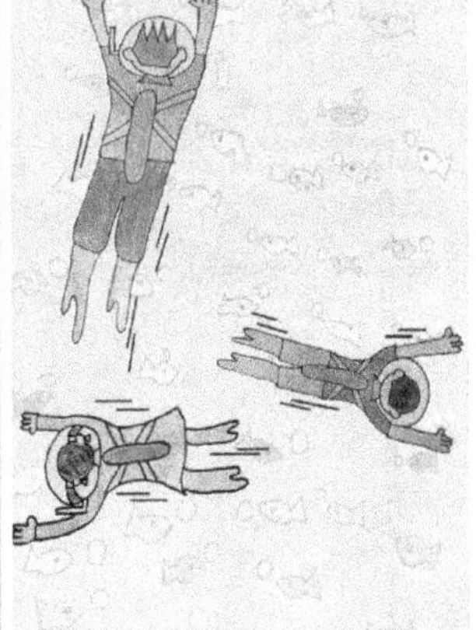

Ram understood the plan of Moly and asked both of them to hide somewhere.

Afsa could not believe her eyes!. All three of them vanished!.

Afsa's army will not do anything without her orders.

"You fools! go and catch them! - screamed Afsa

Three of them from the army went in search of Aadhi, Ram, and Nidhi.

Aadhi found a rock as a place to hide.

Aadhi suddenly felt that somebody was standing next to him.

Aadhi saw the Shark and started screaming out of fear!

Before the Shark could react, Aadhi started swimming faster to escape from there.

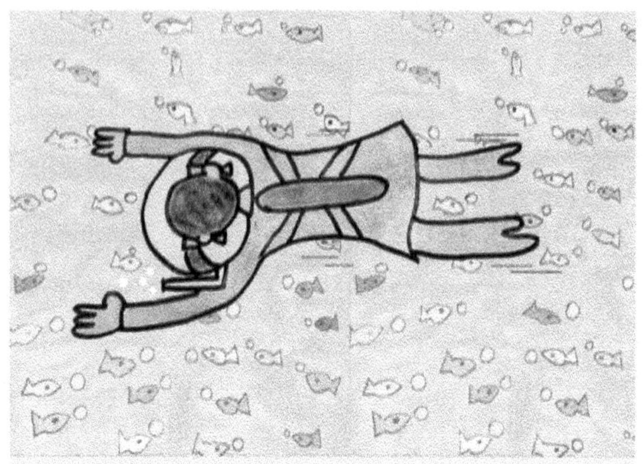

In the meantime, Nidhi was swimming faster to hide somewhere.

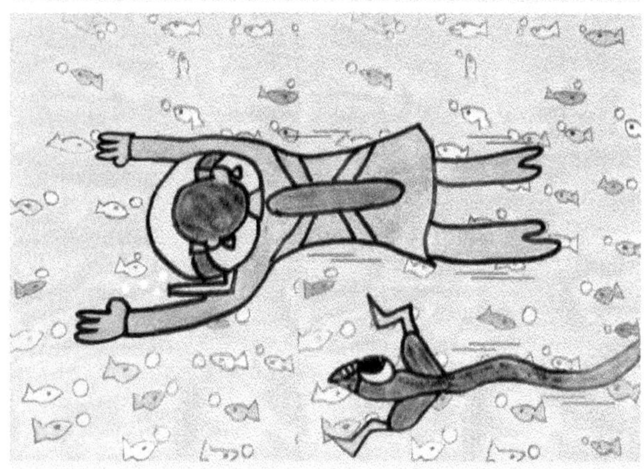

She did not notice an Eel was approaching her.

Eel toucher her and Nidhi were easily shocked!

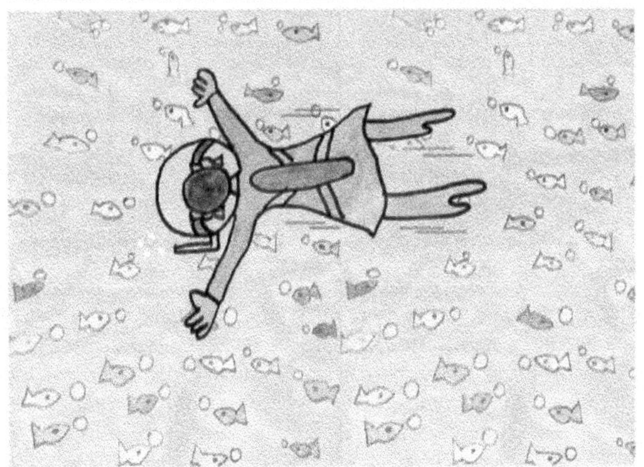

Nidhi fell far away because of the shock but gained consciousness before the Eel could find her. She started swimming faster.

Ram was trying to find a place to hide as he was scared. He did not notice the Turtle at his back.

Ram and the Turtle collided with each other!.

Ram got scared when the Turtle evilly smiled at him.

Before the Turtle was trying to catch him, Ram started swimming faster.

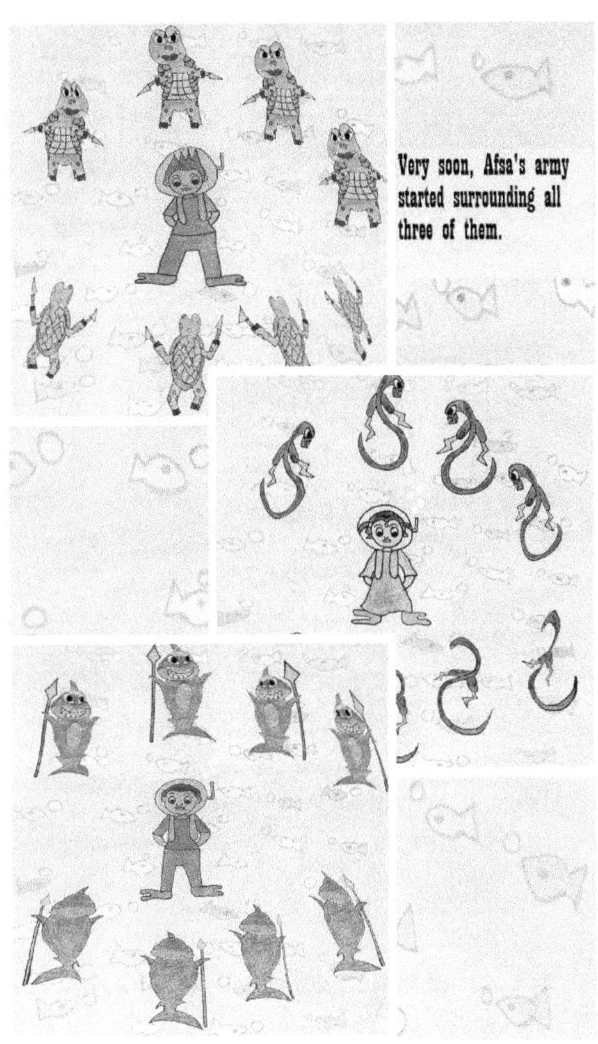
Very soon, Afsa's army
started surrounding all
three of them.

Moly whistled, and all the Sharks turned around to look at her.
FWEEETT
Aadhi smiled and started swimming before the Sharks could notice.

Eel's army started approaching
Nidhi to catch her.
All the Eels collided with each other as Nidhi quickly jumped up!
SHOCK!
SHOCK!
Nidhi smiled and started swimming
away from that place.

Ram was searching for something to attack the Turtles, but he found only a bar of chocolate from his pocket.

Ram saw smiles in all the Turtles' faces.

"These Turtles love chocolate!" - said Moly.

Ram happily dropped the chocolate to distract the Turtles and moved away.

All three of them came together.

"Look, there is a cave!. Let us go inside to hide" - said Ram

All three of them started swimming to reach the cave.

Before they realized it is a Blue Whale, it swallowed them and started moving.

Moly followed the Blue Whale.

Blue Whale took Aadhi, Ram, and Nidhi to the castle of Afsa. Moly followed and reached along with them. Now they are in serious trouble!.

"All three of them should cook for me. I want to taste human food." - ordered Afsa to her army. Afsa's army took them to the kitchen.

Many people were working very hard in the castle, and three of them were shocked to see their state.

Afsa's army attacked their ship and brought these people here.

If they go beyond the Orange Shield, which is around the castle, they will not be able to breathe and will die.

If they don't work, Afsa's army will not let the people inside the castle.

Since they do not want to die, they obey all her orders and work very hard.

But you guys can dis-obey as you have oxygen masks. Do not work at all, and Afsa will ask you to leave the castle. You can get back to your home.

Thanks, Moly!. Let us prepare some Halwa for Afsa and teach her a lesson.

What if she likes Halwa and asks us to stay here only?

We are going to prepare Halwa* with chilly powder.

All of them understood the plan and started preparing Halwa with chilly powder.

* Halwa is a popular dessert in India

Afza took the Halwa from Aadhi and started eating it.

Her mouth started burning like hell. She was screaming and did not know that drinking water can control the burning sensation.

"We will feed you with more Halwa if you are not going to release these people." - said Aadhi angrily.

Afza was not in her senses and did not know how to react. At that moment, she said yes to release the people.

People were not able to believe what just happened!. They started celebrating and praising the kids.

Aadhi, Ram, and Nidhi know who the real hero is!. They thanked Moly.

As per Afsa's order, Blue Whale came to take all of them to the seashore.

Blue Whale started swimming towards the seashore with all the people and the kids.

All three of them started celebrating as soon as they reached the seashore.

Uncle Manu was waiting at the seashore. He was excited and felt proud after listening to their adventure.

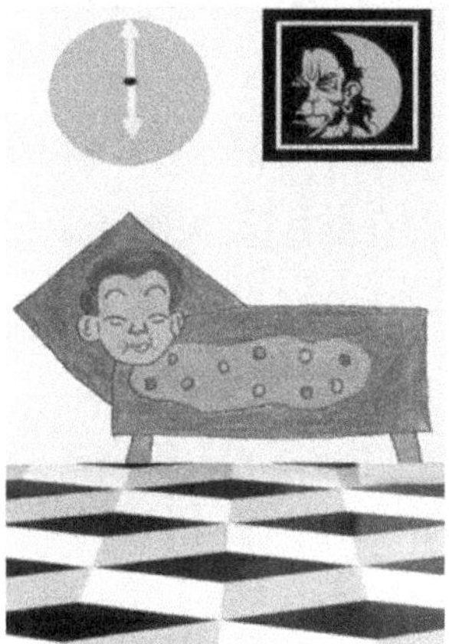

"Wake up!. It is 6'o clock in the morning". - said Aadhi's mother.

Aadhi woke up with a bright smile and started telling his mother about the dream.

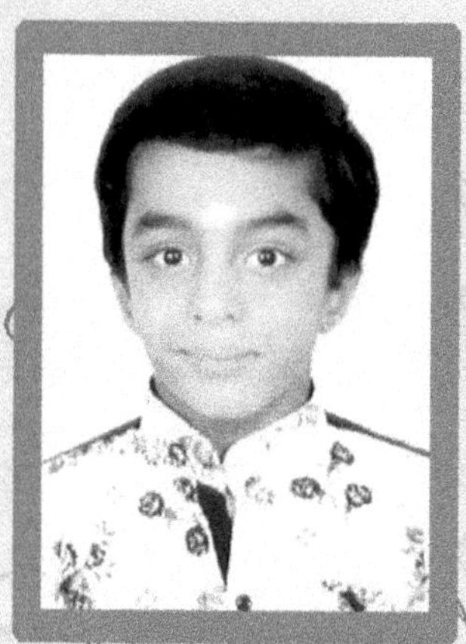

ABOUT THE AUTHOR

Adithya is eight years old. He is studying in Bhavans Vidya Mandir. All the characters in this story are of his own imagination. He took three months to complete this book as he has to draw 100+ images without any reference. The characters Ram and Nidhi are his relatives.

www.ingramcontent.com/pod-product-compliance
Ingram Content Group UK Ltd.
Pitfield, Milton Keynes, MK11 3LW, UK
UKHW021643190726
13853UKWH00001B/31

9 789390 034697